"THIS IS COM
THE LEVEL (
THOSE WHO
BATTLE OF T
SURVIVED—WILL NEVER FORGET IT.
THOSE WHO WERE NOT SHOULD
RE-LIVE IT IN THIS NOVEL. THEY WILL
NEVER FORGET IT."

John Barkham Reviews

Docker stood at the edge of the precipice where the overhang was topped and spiked with bracken and frozen thornbushes. He swept the valley with his binoculars, holding the scopes on an area where the fir trees swayed and bent underneath layers of fog. Lowering the glasses, he listened to distant grinding sounds that shook the ground beneath him. Something massive and powerful broke through a screen of trees a quarter of a mile from them, and Docker said, "Jesus Christ!" as he saw the dark shape of a tank. The tank clawed through the frozen timber toward the slopes, stopping in a grove of trees glittering with hoarfrost and ice. The tank was the most dangerous ground weapon in the German arsenal—a King Tiger Mark II. A Mark II was an awesome sight under any circumstances, and the way it seemed to be hiding in the cover of the mist and trees charged it with an additional, an almost unnatural menace, as if it were more than a great engine of war but rather some species of intelligent, invincible beast . . .